Covered in Armor
With Pay Ru

Dedication

This book is dedicated to my first grandson
Payten Russell. May you always be a ninja
and may all your battles be won with great victory!

"He trains my hands for war and my fingers
fingers for battle." Psalm 144:1

It was a sunny afternoon and Pay Ru was standing

on the deck at his house. He began doing the

stretches he does to get ready for martial arts.

He went over each stretch just as he

would in his class trying to reach further and

further as he pulled.

He could hear the voice of his instructor going over in his head "no pain, no gain, stretch those legs wider!" Pay Ru knows this is true. The farther you can do the splits with your legs the higher you can kick, and high kicking is the goal of every martial artist. You never know when you will need to be able to take out a very tall villain!

Pay Ru had always loved martial arts. He would dream of flying through the air doing a perfect side kick taking out the bad guy right before he could hurt anyone.

He studied so hard never missing a class. When he would be at home he would practice over and over doing each move he had learnt in class, dreaming of one day being as good as Mr. Jung.

Mr. Jung, Pay Ru's martial arts instructor was one of the best in the whole country. Mr. Jung loved teaching martial arts. He taught with so much passion. Mr. Jung not only taught the skills of martial arts but also the keys to living a victorious Christian life. Put the two together and you have a brave Christian ninja!

"Ok my student ninjas, in this week's assignment we will learn how to do a jumping front kick. This is where you stand, jump up and kick forward. In other words you don't back up from your problem but you jump forward in faith believing you will overcome!

Mr. Jung said "we will also memorize Ephesians 6:11 "put on the full armor of God, so that you will be able to stand firm against the schemes of the Devil." It is so important that we learn to put on the full armor of God. Then we will be ready for whatever the devil may hit us with. Learning a jumping front kick will prepare us for physical attacks directly in front of us." Pay Ru stood in attention listening to Mr. Jung. "I will be a brave ninja fully clothed in the armor of God and ready for any tricks the devil may throw at me!" Pay Ru thought.

"Let's see what the armor of God consists of" said

Mr. Jung. "The helmet of salvation, the belt of

truth, the breastplate of righteousness, the shield

of faith, feet covered in preparation of the gospel

of peace, and then there is the sword of the

spirit. It sounds to me like your whole

body is covered."

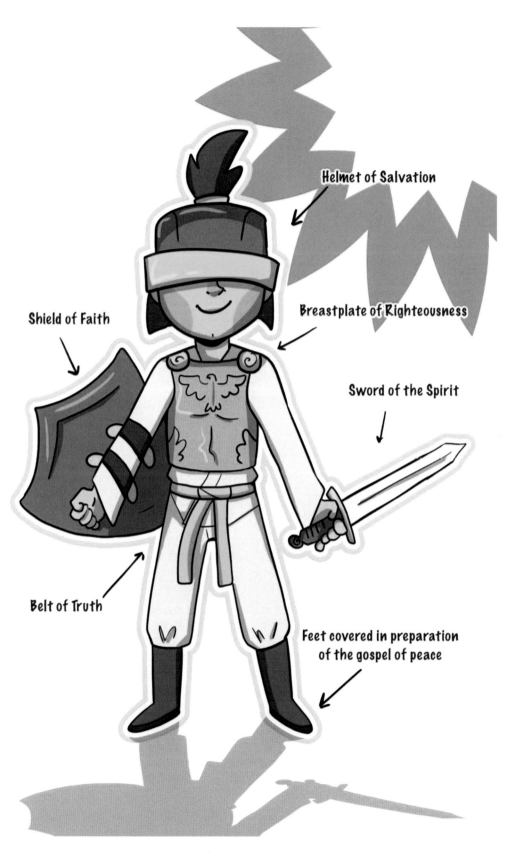

Helmet of Salvation

Shield of Faith

Breastplate of Righteousness

Sword of the Spirit

Belt of Truth

Feet covered in preparation
of the gospel of peace

Pay Ru stood tall in attention raising his hand to

ask a question, "Mr. Jung what does that mean?"

"Well" Mr. Jung said "The helmet covers your mind

So that your thoughts are pure before God.

The belt of truth means that you are truthful in

matters as well as knowing the truth

that God loves you.

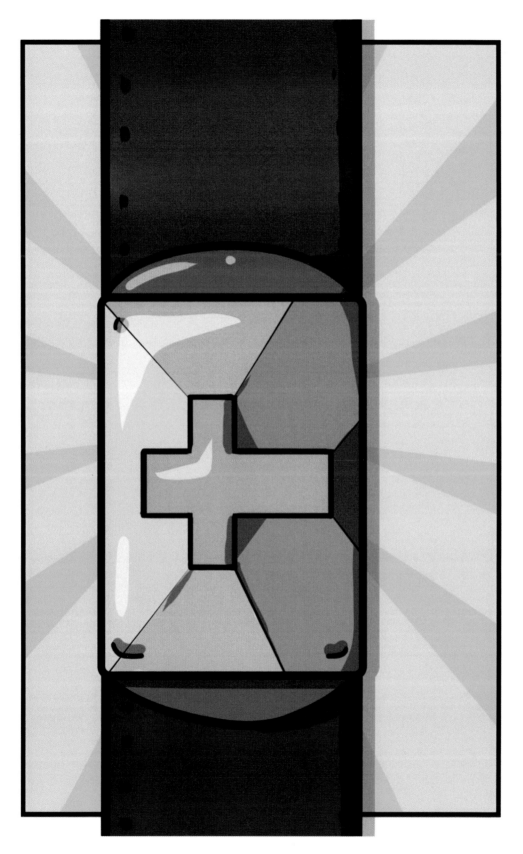

The breastplate of righteousness would mean that

you have a heart for the right things in life

as well as for God.

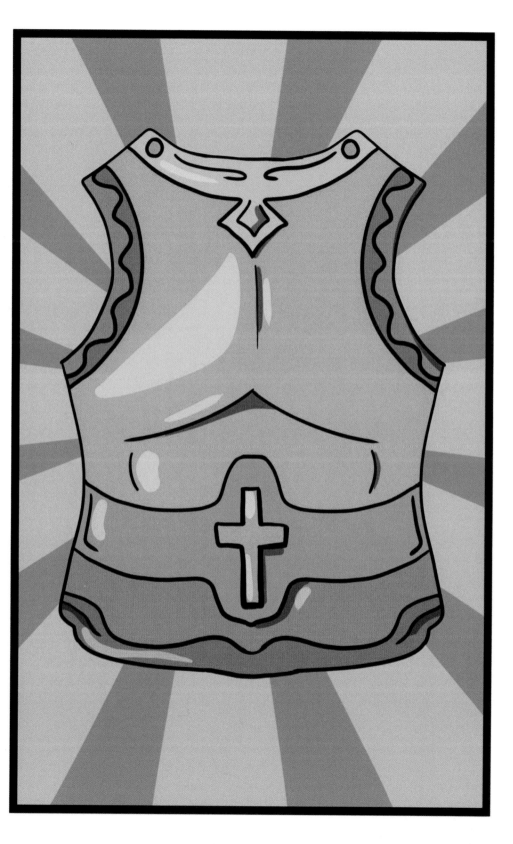

The shield of faith covers us against the devils

arrows of attack. Because we believe in God our

faith keeps us standing when bad things come.

Then there is the sword of the spirit. This is the word of God which is true and we can use God's promises in the bible like a sword against the devil.

"Oh yeah, then our feet should be shod with the preparation of the gospel of peace. This means we should be busy sharing the good news of God's love to the world. God doesn't love just one person but the whole world and we need to tell everyone."

Mr. Jung said.

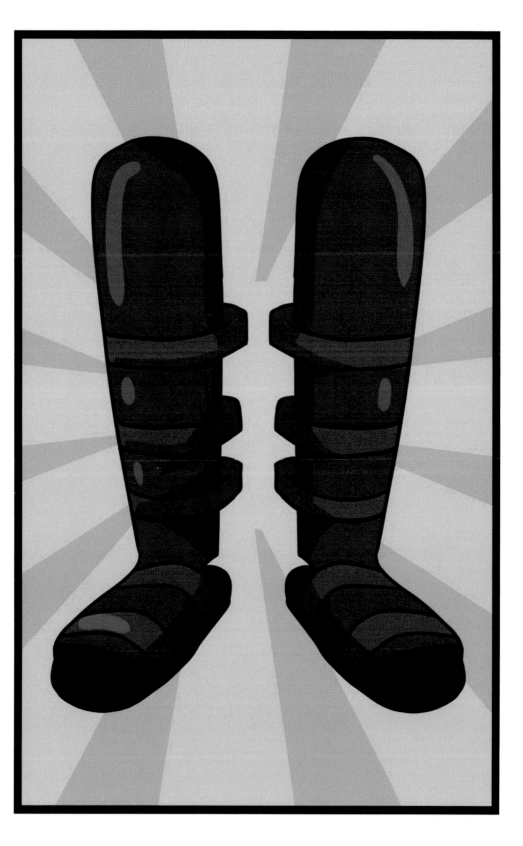

Pay Ru had a huge smile come across his face. He was going to tell everyone he knew how much Jesus loves them. Something this good needed to be shared with the whole world! It was possible to be a ninja and a child of the King! God loves all of us and accepting His gift of eternal life is simple.

Mr. Jung asked Pay Ru "Have you received God's

gift of eternal life? Pay Ru thought for a minute.

He remembered one night when he 7 years old his

dad had asked him the same question.

Pay Ru's dad led him in a simple prayer like this. "Jesus, I want you to come and live in my heart. Please forgive my sins. I accept you as Lord of my life." Pay Ru looked up at Mr. Jung and said with a big bold voice "Yes Sir! I have and I will share the good news with all my friends."

If we wear our armor we can be ready for

anything. Just like Mr. Jung, Pay Ru was a

mighty ninja clothed from head to toe not

only in armor but he was also ready

for eternity!

The End

Made in the
USA
Columbia, SC